# McNally's

# PUZZLE

G·K
Hall
&Co.

*Also by Lawrence Sanders*
*in Large Print:*

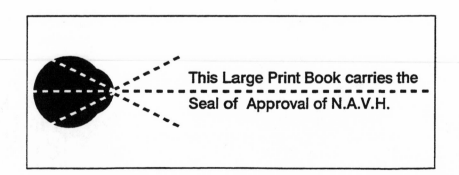

This Large Print Book carries the
Seal of Approval of N.A.V.H.

# McNally's

# P U Z Z L E

## Lawrence Sanders

G.K. Hall & Co.
Thorndike, Maine

Published in 1996 by arrangement with G.P. Putnam's Sons.

G.K. Hall Large Print Core Collection.

The text of this Large Print edition is unabridged.
Other aspects of the book may vary from the original edition.

Set in 16 pt. News Plantin.

Printed in the United States on permanent paper.

**Library of Congress Cataloging in Publication Data**

Sanders, Lawrence, 1920–
    McNally's puzzle / Lawrence Sanders.
        p.    cm.
    ISBN 0-7838-1712-6 (lg. print : hc)
    ISBN 0-7838-1713-4 (lg. print : sc)
    1.  McNally, Archy (Fictitious character) — Fiction.
2.  Private investigators — Forida — Palm Beach — Fiction.
3.  Palm Beach (Fla.) — Fiction. 4.  Large type books.
I.  Title.
[PS3569.A5125M357   1996b]
813'.54—dc20                                                    96-5398